Amelia's

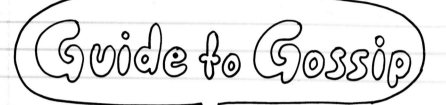
Guide to Gossip

The Good, the Bad, and the Ugly

by Marissa Moss
(and master storyteller Amelia)

Simon & Schuster Books for Young Readers

New York   London   Toronto   Sydney

Wow! The rumors are spreading FAR!

This guide is dedicated to
Elias, Shelah, and Debbie,
all expert gossips.

SIMON & SCHUSTER BOOKS FOR YOUNG READERS
An imprint of Simon & Schuster Children's Publishing Division
1230 Avenue of the Americas, New York, New York 10020
Copyright © 2006 by Marissa Moss

A Paula Wiseman Book

SIMON & SCHUSTER BOOKS FOR YOUNG READERS
is a trademark of Simon & Schuster, Inc.

Don't
believe a
word you
hear unless
you trust
the source!

Amelia® and the notebook design are
registered trademarks of Marissa Moss.

Book design by Amelia
(with help from Lucy Ruth Cummins)

The text for this book is hand-lettered.
Manufactured in China

NOT an urban
legend — it's
true!

2 4 6 8 10 9 7 5 3 1

CIP data for this book is available from the Library
of Congress.
ISBN-13: 978-1-4169-1475-4
ISBN-10: 1-4169-1475-7

No idle
gossips here!

* first
edition *

Amelia's

Guide to Gossip

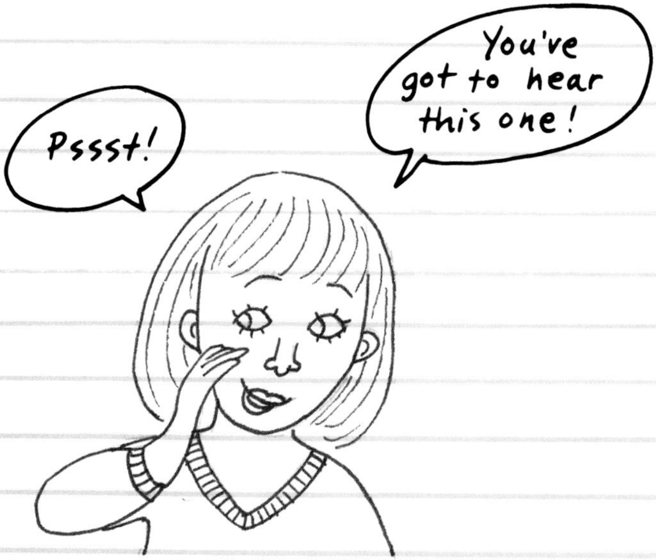

G

G is for
Guess what's new!

G is for
Gotta hear
this!

G is for
Gab!

is for Gossip – and it's also for Guide, so this is a Double G notebook. I'm pretty good at guidebooks (this is my fourth – I've also made a Boredom Survival Guide, School Survival Guide, and Bully Survival Guide). But I'm not so good at gossip. I figure writing a guide like this will turn me into an instant expert. I want to know how to survive gossip (when it's about me) but also how to tell when it's true or not, how to enjoy it without getting into trouble, and how to turn an ordinary story into hot, juicy gossip.

Gossip can be like fire – mesmerizing to watch, but if you get too close, you can get burned. →

And if you're on the wrong side of it, you'll get smoke in your eyes. ↙

Like today — I heard this rumor and I wasn't sure if I believed it or not. Either way, I had to tell my best friend, Carly.

me
↓

Carly
↓

Did you hear about this? My English teacher, Mr. Lambaste, keeps handcuffs in the locked drawer of his desk and he uses them on students!

If you're bad — or if he just doesn't like you — he gives you detention in his room and handcuffs you to your desk for an hour!

Come on, Amelia! You believe that? He's mean, but not _that_ mean.

Yes, he is!

Then he would have done that to _you_ that time he gave you detention.

Maybe they're new — he just got them. Or maybe I was lucky and he forgot to use them.

"Besides," Carly argued, "that's illegal."

"Like he cares!" I scoffed.

"He doesn't want to get arrested or lose his job." Carly's always so calm about these sorts of things. I get all excited and she stays steady and practical. It's one of the things I love about her — but sometimes it can be exasperating.

So I kept on arguing back, in favor of the gossip. Really, it was too good _not_ to be true.

"Aha!" I said.

"Aha, what?" she asked.

"You didn't say it's something he _wouldn't_ do because he's not that horrible, just that he wouldn't want to get into trouble for it. That kind of rumor rings true because it fits — it fits Mr. L. perfectly!"

Even if some gossip isn't true, it can have an emotional truth to it. It can feel absolutely right! ↓

Carly's lucky because she has a normal English teacher. →

I'm stuck with Mr. L., who's always telling me what a bad student I am. He thinks I tried to poison him once with homemade cookies — that's how suspicious he is! ←

"Okay," Carly admitted. "You're right about that, but it still doesn't make the gossip true. This isn't news you're talking about — it's still gossip. Mean gossip."

Sometimes the line between news and gossip seems pretty thin to me.

"You shouldn't spread gossip unless it's true," she added.

"Then it would be all right?" I asked. "You said before that it's never nice."

Carly shrugged. "It's never nice, but it's a million times worse if you're telling lies."

In the case of Mr. L, I think it's doing other students a favor to let them know he's like this with everyone. Otherwise, they might worry they really were bad students. Really, he's just a bad teacher. →

I was relieved to find out that I wasn't the only kid he insulted. Not that I wanted someone else to suffer — I just needed to know it wasn't my fault — he likes to pick on kids. It's almost his hobby. ↙

And some gossip, even if it's true, you can't repeat or you'll get into trouble. Like a girl was sending nasty anonymous e-mails – REALLY mean stuff. Everyone knew about it, but no one wanted to be a rat and tell on her. We still talked about her to each other, but NOT to grown-ups.

Gossiping about her to other kids actually helped people. Like the rumors about Mr. L., it was a kind of warning. Of course, sometimes gossip is just fun, not at all educational, but if it doesn't hurt anybody, isn't that okay?

Carly says it <u>always</u> hurts the person being talked about because what makes gossip g<u>oss</u>ip is that it's about things people <u>don't</u> want known. Or it's personal comments that aren't nice. Saying "She's such a good artist!" isn't gossip, but saying "She draws on bathroom walls!" is. Sometimes it's hard to tell the difference.

Trust me – sometimes rumors NEED to be spread.

This is one of those times.

What's your source? Maybe you didn't hear right.

I trust you. I just don't trust the rumor.

I heard right — I'm sure of it. But Carly has a point. Sometimes a simple sentence can get really twisted when it passes from person to person, like in the game telephone, where you whisper something into someone's ear, they do the same, and with the last person you see how you end up with a completely different sentence than was started with.

That gives me an idea – here's a simple sentence test. Knowing that the rumor has been garbled and changed, pick which sentence you think is the original piece of gossip.

1. Sue's sadder legend quashed the fact.

a) Sue had a hunch and washed her hat.

b) Sue spat out her lunch and splashed the cat.

c) Sue sat on her lunch and squashed it flat.

2. Liam's locker smells like cold meat sandwiches half-filled with dog hair.

a) Liam's locker smells like bony old witches have gone to dye hair.

b) Liam's locker smells like old feet and ditches half-full of diapers.

c) Liam's locker smells like bologna sandwiches have gone to die there.

3. Maya sorted hairy budget sandpaper.
ⓐ Maya ordered magic card presents.
Surprise!
ⓑ Maya has suddenly smudged handprints.
Yucch!
ⓒ Maya has ordinary midget grandparents.
We love you, dear!

4. Hillary collects thread.
ⓐ Hillary stole Wesley's bed.
Mine!
ⓑ Hillary sweats real bad.
ⓒ Hillary still wets the bed.
What's that wet spot?

Answers:

If you picked mostly a's, you need to get your hearing checked.

If you picked mostly b's, you need to get your sense of logic checked.

If you picked mostly c's, you don't need to get anything checked — you have great gossip intuition and can tell the real thing from a muddled mess.

You mean "Maya has ordinary midget grandparents" is the real gossip? Are you sure? Sounds like mixed-up nonsense to me and I have a great nose for gossip.

But do you have a great _ear_ for gossip? Remember, gossip isn't necessarily _true_ information — it's gossip!

Which brings me back to what Carly said before — how do you know if a rumor is true? And does it have to be <u>literally</u> true or just true in a general, vague way (like Mr. L. is mean to kids even if he doesn't actually handcuff them)?

Carly says some gossip is like watching clouds — it can change shape right before your eyes. One minute you're looking at a dragon, the next a giant floating ice-cream cone. I think it's more like quicksand — the more you search for solid ground to stand on, the farther you sink.

Up to my ears in slippery, shifting gossip.
↓

Help!

There are different levels of shiftiness, different degrees of probability. All you need is a scale to measure each particular piece of gossip to give you a sense of whether it's likely to be true or not.

Rumor Reading

Measure for Saturated Levels of Lies

10 — Totally provable — not a rumor at all, but a fact.
Example: Most kids don't like vegetables.

8 — Highly plausible, but not yet substantiated.
Example: The principal puts a black mark by the name of every kid who's had detention.

6 — Could be, but doesn't seem too likely.
Example: Locker 1313 is jinxed — if you put anything into it and shut the door, it disappears FOREVER!

4 — Nope, don't buy it.
Example: Cafeteria food is nutritious and delicious.

2 — Who are you trying to fool?
Example: The principal is cancelling P.E. for the rest of the year and replacing it with film criticism — watch as many movies as you like!

0 — Are you CRAZY?
Example: The most popular girl in school is Cleo.

Or you can use the Gossip Probability Factor Test.

1. Something is probably true if...

| @ ...you hear the same thing from three different people. | ⓑ ...the whole school knows the rumor by the end of the day. | © ...you've never, ever heard anything like it before. |

you've already heard this?.

Can I tell you anyway?

Enough already!

WOW!!

2. Something is probably made up if...

| @ ... a celebrity, a brand name, or an elf is involved. | ⓑ ... people laugh when they hear it. | © ...it reminds you of a movie you just saw. |

It's just not true!

you're kidding, right?

This is strangely familiar.

3. Something is based on some kernel of fact, even if it's exaggerated, if...

ⓐ... you know for sure part of it is true.	ⓑ...other people know for sure some part of it is true.	ⓒ... it just sounds true.

Well, she does have a jellyroll nose.

He did eat pizza for lunch— I saw him!

How can I NOT believe it?

4. Something is definitely not true, even if part of it is based on facts, if...

ⓐ... it involves an alien.	ⓑ... it involves a buried treasure.	ⓒ...it involves a ghost, vampire, or werewolf.

I want to learn how to graph a parabola.

Come on, you know you WANT it to be true!

I'm the creak you hear in the bathroom pipes!

Answers:
  If the rumor fits mostly a's, it could very well be true. You can tell it to as many people as you want.

  If the rumor fits mostly b's, it probably isn't true, but it still could be. If it's entertaining enough, go ahead and pass it on.

  If the rumor fits mostly c's, there's a strong chance it's completely false. You can repeat it only if you warn people that it's not 100% fact (and it might not even be 1% fact). If it's interesting enough, no one will care about the made-up part.

Like the rumor the french fries in the school cafeteria are 30% cardboard, 20% eraser shavings, 10% salt, and 40% fat— the percentages might not be exact and there may actually be some potato involved, but the general idea is accurate enough.

yom! Dig in! ⟶

That tested the gossip. Now here's a test about you — your ability to tell good gossip from sour, rotting drivel.

1. You consider something is probably true if...

ⓐ ... everyone says it.

ⓑ ... it smells right to you.

ⓒ ... no one else believes it.

2. You consider something is not true if...

ⓐ ... no one else believes it.

ⓑ ... it smells fishy to you.

ⓒ ... everyone says it.

3. You consider a rumor to be based on some kernel of fact, even if it's exaggerated, if...
a ... the cool kids say it.
Okay, something is true here.
Wow!
Psst!
Can you believe it?
b ... it has no smell at all.
It doesn't stink.
Sniff!
Sniff!
c ... no one believes it.
Do I see something no one else does? I am unique, after all.
No way!
Can't be!

4. You are totally confused and have no idea what to think if...
a ... the almost-cool kids say it.
Should I follow the crowd?
Listen!
Did you hear?
It's hot!
What to do?
b ... the smelly kids say it.
Maybe it's just old gossip.
c ... only the nerds say it.
I could stand out from the crowd.
No way!
Total bull!

5. You believe gossip that contains at least one of these elements:

ⓐ kissing	ⓑ aliens	ⓒ secret identities

6. You <u>don't</u> believe gossip that contains at least one of these elements:

ⓐ aliens	ⓑ secret identities	ⓒ kissing

7. You trust gossip depending on the...
a ...source.
Well, since YOU said it, how can I not believe it?
b ...freshness.
Nope - it's past the expiration date.
It's still tasty!
c ...number of times it's been repeated.
I've heard this same rumor 68 times now!

8. You automatically don't trust gossip if...
a ... someone you hate tells it to you.
True or not, I don't want to believe it.
b ... the person who tells you hesitates a lot.
Then he said... hmmm... what was it? Oh yeah, he said he really liked her. And... um... well... he was going to... something. I forget exactly what.
c ... the person who tells you is notorious for mixing up facts.
Believe me, she asked him out. Unless it was the other way around. Let me think...

Answers:

If you chose mostly a's, you need to learn to think for yourself instead of always following the crowd. Either that or you love gossip so much, you want it all to be true.

If you chose mostly b's, you're an independent thinker with a keen sense of smell and a nose for news. Does that make you accurate in judging whether gossip is true or false? I have no idea!

If you chose mostly c's, you like to stand out from the crowd. Either that or you just don't trust gossip, no matter how probable it is.

If you chose a complete mix of a's, b's, and c's, you're as confused about gossip and how true it is as I am — sorry, I can't help you!

you can always use the coin flipping method when in doubt — heads, it's true, tails, it's false.

I cannot tell a lie.

The thing is, sometimes it doesn't matter if gossip is true or not — it's just a lot of fun. <u>That's</u> something Carly agrees with me on. We just don't always see eye to eye on what makes a great gossip item. Carly likes stories about famous people — the kind you see in magazines at the supermarket checkout stand.

Those are okay, but I like better the amazing stories about ordinary people — another kind of thing you see at the checkout stand.

Those are stories you can really sink your teeth into!
It doesn't matter that they're obviously nowhere near true—
in fact, that's part of what makes them so fun.

Carly wants to be a reporter when she grows up — like
my dad. Usually she talks about being an investigative
reporter, but sometimes she imagines what it would be like
to write for one of those kinds of newspapers. Myself, I
like inventing stories, not presenting information (that's
boooooring), but I'd have fun being a reporter for
gossip rags. We made our own once for school and
called it "The Daily Dish."

The Daily Dish
All the news that's fit to make up.

Cafeteria Serves Radioactive Waste:
Glowing Spinach Tips off Science Teacher to Hazard

"I always had my suspicions," Ms. Reilly said. "The food there smelled strange, like chemicals rather than something edible." The cook refused to comment on the allegations.

Lost and Found: the Twilight Zone!

Objects go in, but they never come out! The growing, moldering pile of jackets, shoes, socks, notebooks, backpacks, lunch bags, umbrellas, books, pens, calculators, and all other objects turned in to the Lost and Found are never seen again once they're put into the black hole of a closet. Once there, they all blend together.

GIANT EVIL DUST BUNNIES

Mildred Borstein never vacuumed under her bed, allowing the dust bunnies there to grow to monstrous proportions. Small stuffed animals that fell off the bed were devoured in seconds. The dust bunnies are now so large, they have taken over the 12-year-old's room, growling and snapping at anyone who tries to enter.

"I guess I'll have to sleep on the couch until I go to college," the girl shrugged, resigned to her homeless fate. Her mother, however, has not given up, and is planning a sneak attack tonight.

COCKROACH INFESTATION IN SCIENCE LAB

In an experiment gone horribly awry, eighteen large hissing cockroaches escaped from their cages and have now spread through the entire Math-Science wing. Impervious to poison or traps, the roaches now freely roam wild and have been seen in lockers, bathrooms, and drinking fountains. Students are advised to inspect food before eating it in case a cockroach is hiding there.

Normally, printed gossip has more weight and authority than the spoken kind — especially if there are photos. But I don't think anyone believed the stories we made up for The Daily Dish. That's okay — we didn't expect them to. It was just fun dreaming them up and then doctoring photos to go along with them. I wanted to do a special edition on urban legends, but Carly said those kinds of stories have been around so long, people actually believe them now (or kind of halfheartedly believe them), figuring there must be some truth to them if they've survived for so long. I still think they're gossip, just very old gossip that somehow never goes stale.

Most gossip has a very short shelf life.
↓

Not urban legends — they can live for years, even decades.
↓

Consume now while still juicy! →

Best when used by next week

Did Cleo really kiss Justin? Open the bag to find out!

Did a boy find a rat in his order of fried chicken? Open now for the answer!

Stay-fresh package keeps crisp for ages!
←

Urban Legends

Moldy oldies we all have heard ↓

↑ the lady who finds a thumb in her bowl of soup

"Where can I drop you off? Hey, where'd you go?"

↑ the hitchhiker who turns out to be a ghost

"If the phone hadn't rung just then, I'd never have escaped the fire! It had to be my guardian angel!"

"I knew she really loved me— I knew it! Now I can die in peace."

↑ the letter lost in the mail for decades that is finally delivered at just the right moment

↑ the mysterious phone call that saves a life

There used to be a show on TV called "Fact or Fiction" that I loved to watch. It basically had a bunch of different stories — some urban legends, some true, some invented. At the end of the show you were supposed to guess which ones were invented and which were real. The thing is, the real stories seemed so fake, you'd never guess they actually happened. That's what made the show so cool — the real stuff was as unbelievable as the fiction.

Now with my handy-dandy gossip machine you can turn dry, boring day-to-day facts into the MOST EXCITING, UNUSUAL, DRAMATIC EVENTS POSSIBLE (as shown on TV in "Fact or Fiction")! Embroidery often does the trick — add new bits onto the old to make the dullest occurrence a sparkly adventure.

add bric-a-brac ↓

Old fact:
Maya fell and broke her ankle.

sew on fancy buttons ↓

New, improved version:
Maya was chasing after a bank robber and had almost caught him when he threw a heavy bag of coins at her. She tripped over the bag, fell flat on her face, and broke her ankle. The robber got away, but it turned out the bag was full of rare coins, way more valuable than the rest of the money the thief kept.

glue on glitter and sequins ↘

tie on ribbons and bows ↓

The bank was so happy to get the coins back, they gave Maya a reward for returning them, even if it was by accident.

I'm a hero!

Old fact:
Max spent the weekend visiting his dad now that his parents are separated.

New, improved fact:
Max's dad is in the FBI witness protection program and had to leave his family and move away. He's completely changed his identity with a new name, dyed hair, and a phony accent. Max waits at a designated corner until a strange car drives by and whisks him away to the secret location where his dad is now.

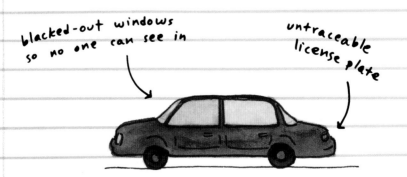

See, that stuff makes good gossip. The lowest level of rumors is the kind that's local – just in your school or family. But that can be the most interesting kind too, because you know the people involved. (Celebrities are people you think you know, but really you don't – you just know <u>about</u> them.)

The fresh gossip at school now is about the girl with the mean e-mails. Somehow the principal found out and we had to sit through a long, boooooring assembly about NOT misusing e-mail. Everyone's talking about WHO told on the girl. No one knows, so a lot of different names are being suggested. That's not real gossip – it's speculation.

School has the MOST gossip, but there's a lot in families too. No matter who is in the family, chances are there's gossip about:

① The Black Sheep – Baaa!
   The person who didn't live up to
   expectations. They don't even have to be a
   criminal, just not the doctor everyone wanted.

② The Skeleton in the Closet –
   The secret everyone tries to hide.
   Boo!

It can be something really small, like Grandpa was married before and divorced wife #1, who is NEVER mentioned. Or it can be something really big, like Grandpa was married before Grandma to three different women and he didn't divorce any of them. Uh-oh! Grandpa's a bigamist.

③ The Buried Treasure —

Something of value that everyone in the family wants. Again, it could be something small, like Grandma's teapot. Or it could be something huge, like the family farm and 362 acres.

The best gossip needs to be both juicy and satisfying. Juicy gossip has some illicit tinge to it — the thrill of supersecretive stuff. Satisfying gossip isn't necessarily great gossip by itself but because of _who_ it's about. There's something about the gossip that contradicts how the person acts or seems — which is EXACTLY what makes it so satisfying.

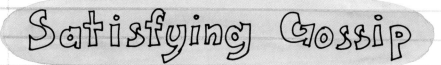

Satisfying Gossip

Mom is a total book snob — she says she only reads great classics or informative nonfiction, NEVER junk. But I happen to know that her lowest dresser drawer is _full_ of cheap romance novels — the kind whose authors have names like Violet LaVoile or Star Meadows. This is JUICY and SATISFYING family gossip I'd love to tell _someone_, but if I did, Mom would kill me. (And that's NOT satisfying.)

> I can't put this book down — it's so exciting!

> There's nothing like reading the history of escalators.

Carly is a health food nut. She makes her mom buy organic groceries and she NEVER eats fast food. But I know she has a weakness for chocolate-glazed doughnuts. She allows herself one a week, which you would think wouldn't be a big deal, but she would die if anyone else found out.

Really, I only eat doughnuts to save some other poor soul from their fatty, greasy, sugary overload. It's a rescue mission.

Leah always teases people who play video games. She says they have batteries instead of brains and are like rats running through electronic mazes for a piece of virtual cheese. But <u>she's</u> secretly addicted herself.

This isn't <u>my</u> Game Boy — it's my cousin's. And I'm not playing it — I'm just testing it for him. DON'T TOUCH!! You'll mess up my score. I mean, <u>his</u> score. JUST GO AWAY!

Max pretends he doesn't like any girls, but I know he has a crush on Charisse. He sent her a secret valentine, but it ended up in the wrong locker — MINE!

My heart is beating so loudly, I'm sure she hears it. What'll I do? Should I talk to her? What if there's something stuck in my teeth?

That Max is cute — too bad he's not boyfriend material.

Charisse seems absolutely perfect in every possible way. She's pretty and stylish, dresses well, and has a British accent. What else does she need? But she has one fatal flaw — she chews her fingernails. With me that would be no big deal. With most people it wouldn't matter. To her it's a major blot on her image, a glaring defect she always tries to hide. Sometimes Charisse even glues on those fake fingernails. That's how I discovered her secret — one of her nails came out in her sandwich! It freaked me out!

sandwich with fingernail garnish

Here's your very own handy-dandy guide to how hot is hot. RATE THE GOSSIP! Is it really hot, smoking, or mouth-wateringly JUICY?

Off-the-charts explosive! You can't wait to tell everyone you meet. This gossip is so wowzah, the whole world looks different because of it. ⟶

Veeeeery interesting — your ears smoke just listening to it and your teeth tingle waiting to repeat it. ⟶

Okay, you're definitely paying attention. It's a warm little morsel — spicy, but not too hot. ⟶

It's a nice little appetizer and if the subject comes up, you'll probably repeat it. Otherwise you wouldn't bother. ⟶

A puff piece, not weighty enough to fill you up. Completely forgettable. ⟶

Why bother to say this? Who cares? ⟶

Dull, boring, a total yawn. This isn't gossip — it's a shopping list. ⟶

The absolute BEST kind of gossip is crazy stories about people you know **well**, like kids and teachers at school or people in your family. Cleo falls into both those categories, since she's still at my school and she'll always be my older sister (unfortunately).

When I got back from the big family reunion with my dad's family last month, Carly's first question was about Cleo.

> Come on now — dish! What happened with Cleo? Who is this Justin guy?

> You'll never believe it!

It's funny that gossiping is called "dishing" — like you're serving up a delicious tidbit.

yum! Smells spicy! →

‹ ‹ ? ? ? ›

Careful — it's hot, hot, HOT!

CLEO GOSSIP
STOP telling lies about me!
Cleo kissed her own cousin (well, stepcousin)!
Cleo tried to poison a teacher by sneaking salt into his coffee! (Okay—it's not fatal, but it's pretty gaggy.)
Cleo's bikini fell off at Gigi's pool party—accidentally on purpose!
It's NOT true—NONE of it!
Cleo thought she was using spray-on tan stuff, but it was really hair removal spray—that's why she didn't have eyebrows for a couple of months!
Cleo ate the cupcakes left in the school office for Teacher Appreciation Day. Her appetite was NOT appreciated

Cleo is the perfect subject for gossip because no matter what you say about her — the crazier the better — it still sounds like it could be true. Here's a Cleo fact-or-fiction test — see how well you can tell which stuff is made up and which really happened.

① Cleo likes to stick french fries up her nose.
Fact ☐
Fiction ☐

② Cleo once threw up on her science teacher, and he thought she did it on purpose.
Fact ☐
Fiction ☐

Is this some sort of bizarre experiment? I won't give you extra credit!

③ Cleo once went to school wearing her nightgown as an English project, saying she was Lady MacBeth.

Fact ☐

Fiction ☐

④ Cleo almost ran over a P.E. class when she took Mom's car for a practice drive in the school parking lot.

Fact ☐

Fiction ☐

⑤ Cleo dressed up as Madonna for the school talent show and sang "I Did It My Way."

Fact ☐

Fiction ☐

Waaaaaaay!

X-rated: cannot be shown on school property (really it's for your own protection—you wouldn't want to see it anyway, believe me)

⑥ For Cinco de Mayo, Cleo brought salsa to Spanish class that was so spicy, six students ended up in the nurse's office.

Fact ☐

Fiction ☐

Wow! Did the salsa burn a hole in the bowl?

You need a strong stomach for Salsa de Cleo!

If you said 5 questions or more were fiction, you don't know Cleo at all.

If you said 3-4 questions were fiction, you've probably seen my sister in action and have an idea what she's capable of.

If you said only 2 questions were fiction, you know Cleo well! You've got a good nose for the gossipy truth — dish it out while it's hot!

If you said only one question was fiction, why _that_ one? If Cleo did most of those outrageous things, why not all of them? Or did you think the test needed one different answer?

If you said NONE of these questions was fiction, you're a GOSSIP WHIZ and Cleo expert and deserve the Golden Goose Award for Gossip Smarts!

why a goose? Are they gossip experts or just make a lot of noise? →

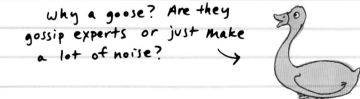

Of course, there's <u>another</u> kind of Cleo gossip — that's not gossip <u>about</u> Cleo but <u>by</u> her. Which is waaaaaay worse because usually it's about ME. That's one reason NEVER to go to the same school as your sister. Luckily my friends all know NOT to believe anything Cleo says. Unluckily that still leaves a lot of kids — and teachers — for her to infect. She's even gossiped about me with kids in Dad's family — cousins I hadn't met, so their first impression of me was through Cleo. Yucch! When that happened, I felt like I needed an extra-strength Cleo disinfectant to wash off the Cleo-colored reputation.

I wanted to scrub away the Cleo stain.

Cleo cleaner

CLEO GOSSIP
(the second kind — by her, not about her)

Lies, lies, ALL LIES!

That's the bad part of gossip — when people spread stories about you that are horrible lies and the more you deny them, the more people think they're true. But if you ignore the rumors, people will _still_ think they're true. So how do you get rid of gossip when it's like stepping on a wad of chewing gum that sticks to the bottom of your shoe no matter how hard you try to scrape it off?

There _are_ ways, but you can't do it alone. You need friends to help you — the more, the better.

How to Stop Gossip
OR RUMOR REMOVAL

no yakking   ① Spread your own rumors   no blabbing
that are exactly the OPPOSITE of whatever the gossip says. The two things will cancel each other out.

② Have as many people as possible spread as many crazy stories as possible so NOTHING will seem believable anymore.

If the stories all intertwine, it's even better — MUCH more confusing.

Lucy is going to be on Teen Idol! She's lucky!

The new kid in French class is really a princess in disguise, like in that movie!

That new French kid is jealous of Lucy being on Teen Idol and tried to poison her so she'd miss the show.

Trevor ate 13 frogs in the science lab. He's gross!

Oh yeah? Well, the P.E. teacher used to work for the CIA interrogating criminals. He's a real torturer.

Did you hear about the P.E. teacher? He still works for the CIA. He's undercover, searching for a kid who hacked into government computers.

I heard that Trevor was trying to save Lucy from being poisoned, so he ate the frogs meant for her.

The new French kid cooked the frogs for Trevor to eat because in France, frogs are a delicacy.

No, you're wrong— Lucy ate the frogs as a stunt to get on TV. She's not on Teen Idol, but Survivor!

That's not what I heard! The frogs weren't cooked — the P.E. teacher scared Trevor so much, he swallowed the frogs thinking they had microchips inside of them. It was all part of the hacking case.

③ If those don't work, wait out the war or go into hiding, wearing camouflage.

Achoo! It's dusty down here!

④ Accept the rumor as true, but turn it into something good.

It was a big sacrifice for Amelia to eat the teachers' candy, but she had the courage to protect them from cavities, bad breath, and sugar highs.

How noble of her! Next time she should share the burden with me!

⑤ Accept the rumor as true, but turn it into something completely unbelievable.

That wasn't Amelia—she was abducted by a UFO and replaced by a fake Amelia who's really an alien trying to infiltrate our society— and eat its chocolate.

Oh, I thought it was Cleo pretending to be Amelia. She's pretty alien, though.

I can't believe this! Just when I'm writing about Rumor Removal, people are REALLY gossiping about me!

And they're not talking about candy. Kids are saying that I'm the one who got the e-mail girl into trouble. But I didn't! Why would I? She didn't send me a mean e-mail. I just heard about it like everyone else. I'm going for option #3 — hiding. If I stay in the library working on this guide, I can wait out the rumor — maybe.

Gossip about kids is one thing. Gossip about teachers is another. I know a lot of stuff gets made up about kids, but somehow the stuff about teachers always seems true, no matter how crazy the rumor. That's because really we kids know NOTHING about teachers except what they tell us and how they act in class. But there's always one student in every school who's got the dirt on all the teachers. If you want to know which teacher eats onion sandwiches for lunch (well, the breath is a BIG hint on this one), which one has a stash of comics in their desk drawer, or which one spends their summers playing in a rock band, you have to   ask the teacher expert.

In my school, that's Gigi. She's Cleo's best friend, but I don't hold that against her — she's still cool.

Don't ask how I know — I just do!

No matter how much you bug her, she won't give away her sources.

MATCH THE TEACHER TO THE GOS[SIP]

Mr. Lambaste

Ms. Oates

Mr. Le Poivre

Ms. Reilly

Mr. Klein

Mrs. Church

Has a second j[ob] being a clown at little kid parties.

Is married to another teacher in the school — who?

Lives alone with 38 cats.

Used to be a hippie, wear tie-dye all the time, and live in a commune.

Claims to have been abducted by a UFO in 1975.

Is going to law school at nights

ANSWERS
(According to expert Gigi)

Mr. Lambaste — Has a second job being a clown at little kid parties.

Ms. Oates — Is married to another teacher in the school—who? (the Spanish teacher, Mr. Ricardo)

Mr. Le Poivre — Lives alone with 38 cats.

Ms. Reilly — Used to be a hippie, wear tie-dye all the time, and live in a commune.

Mr. Klein — Claims to have been abducted by a UFO in 1975.

Mrs. Church — Is going to law school at nights.

Strange but True!

What's the difference between gossip and trivia? If you tell trivia that you know about someone, does the act of telling turn it into gossip? Is gossip more a verb than a noun, or both equally? These are profound philosophical questions. Actually, gossip is all three things — the person who spreads it, the thing being spread, and the act of spreading it. The gossip gossips about gossip — get it? Is there any other word that is so multi-dimensional? Is there another word that can be the subject, the object, and the verb, all in the same sentence?

When I asked Carly about this, she said I was thinking too much.

I can't help thinking about gossip — especially now that it's about <u>me</u>. I'm afraid that once a bad story starts, it can only get <u>worse</u>. I mean, now people say I told on a girl for writing mean e-mails — what will they say <u>next?</u>

Yeah, I can think of another word like that — poop! The poop poops out the poop. See!

Amelia's a spy for the principal. She notices when anyone is late to class and rats on them.

Not only that — I heard the PTA hired her to snoop on kids. Now she's telling PARENTS all our secrets!

She's a complete fink. I heard she put a listening device in all the bathrooms. Watch out what you say there!

What a traitor! Next she'll set up spy cameras everywhere. She's completely sold out to the parents and teachers!

She says she writes in a notebook, but really it's a BLOG! She's spilling our stuff out there for EVERYONE to read!

HELP! I'm squashed...

... by rumors!

And they're lies, all LIES!

Can people really say that stuff? Can they believe it? What if no one will talk to me anymore? How can I rub out the rumors?

The problem is gossip travels in waves that are faster than the speed of light or sound. I can't outrun it or escape it — it's way too speedy.

Here's the proof: An ordinary conversation doesn't go farther than the people speaking to each other — that's the speed of sound. But one juicy whisper can be all over the school by the end of the day — that's the speed of gossip. It's completely unpredictable — saturating one area, leaving another untouched until suddenly EVERYONE's heard it.

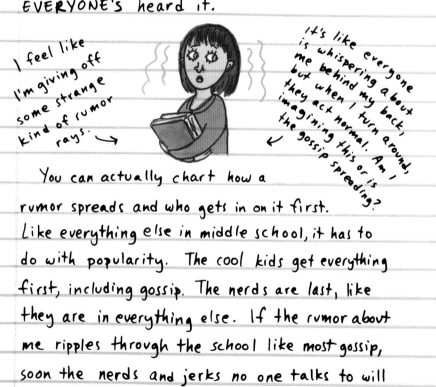

I feel like I'm giving off some strange kind of rumor rays.

It's like everyone is whispering about me behind my back, but when I turn around, they act normal. Am I imagining this or is the gossip spreading?

You can actually chart how a rumor spreads and who gets in on it first. Like everything else in middle school, it has to do with popularity. The cool kids get everything first, including gossip. The nerds are last, like they are in everything else. If the rumor about me ripples through the school like most gossip, soon the nerds and jerks no one talks to will be the only people I can be with — HELP!

The Gossip Ripple

The rumor starts here.

Immediately all the cool, in-the-know kids pick up on it.

The circle of kids who know the cool kids get in on it next.

Even the nerds have heard it out here.

Effect

The kids who aren't popular, but aren't unpopular either, are the biggest group of all. Once they hear it, it's all over the place.

The jerks no one likes or talks to know the rumor by now — they're the last to hear it.

This is a bigger group, so the rumor spreads faster.

Now there's no hope — the rumor is EVERYWHERE! Who ever thought they'd be rippling about ME?

The jocks hear it in this group.

I guess that shows something useful about gossip — not that lies are spread about people (that's DEFINITELY not useful, especially when I'm the person being talked about) — but because gossip holds groups of people together and let's you see who's cool and who isn't. If you're not sure whether someone's a nerd or not (though usually that's VERY obvious), you can find out by seeing how much gossip they know. Or by hearing the kind of gossip that's said about them. So maybe it's good to be talked about. I need to remember that. It all depends on what is being said.

Bad Gossip
(the kind you DON'T want said about you)

Personal Appearance

Where DID Hilary get those shoes? They're from Dorkville!

She always wears the worst things! Have you seen her socks?

Personal Hygiene

That Chris NEVER brushes his teeth — they're green!

EW! GROSS!

Some psychologists actually did a scientific study about gossip (I swear, this is the truth — not a wild rumor!), and they discovered that not only is gossip a useful social tool for figuring out how to fit in with a group, you can learn some valuable lessons from rumors. Even if the actual piece of gossip isn't true, you can learn something from it. So when I'm gossiping, I'm actually expanding my mind. I like that idea!

Of course, when people gossip about <u>me</u>, I want them to learn good stuff, not bad, mean stuff. Maybe the thing they can learn from the rumor about me and the e-mail girl is NOT to trust gossip. That's useful too!

Important School Gossip You Need to Know

① Never buy lunch on Fridays — that's leftover hash day, when they take the food left over during the week, mash it together, and call it Chef's Surprise.

The surprise is that they call this edible.

I told you to bring your lunch on Fridays, but did you listen? No!

The smell alone is enough to kill your stomach.

④ The 3rd toilet stall in the girls' bathroom in the 800 wing is a DISASTER — no one dares to use it.

⑤ Mr. Lambaste is the meanest teacher in the whole school. If you can get out of taking classes with him, DO IT! ANY teacher would be better than him.

See — not only can you learn from gossip, it can save your skin. It's way more useful information than the chart in the back of this notebook, which tells you how many pecks to a bushel or how many scruples to a dram. (I don't even know <u>what</u> those things are!)

Here's the test the researchers gave for YOU to take (along with my answers as examples).

① What is the most interesting gossip you've heard lately?

Hmmm, hard to say. Definitely NOT the one about me (boooring!) and the one about Mr. L. is so predictable, I'm not sure it's interesting. I guess I'd have to say Cleo kissing Justin in the barn at the family reunion.

Kissing is high on any gossip list anyway.

Cleo, puckering up

② Who was the gossip about?

a. a friend or acquaintance (most people said this)

b. a stranger (this was the next most popular answer)

c. a celebrity (celebrity was below stranger, believe it or not)

d. family (the fewest people said this — I'm unusual)

③ Did you pass it on?

a. yes (most people did, of course — me, too!)

b. yes, to more than 3 people (Fewer told this many people, but so far I've told 4 people about Cleo — Carly, Nadia, Leah, and Maya. What's the point of juicy gossip if you don't tell as many people as possible?)

④ Did the gossip reflect badly on the person being talked about?

Most people said yes to this, but in Cleo's case I'm not sure. Kissing is usually good gossip, not bad. And Justin is cute, so that makes it doubly good (for Cleo). But <u>he's</u> kissing <u>Cleo</u> and she's not cute, so that makes it bad (for Justin).

⑤ Did you learn anything that you can apply to your life?

Actually, I learned a few things.

1. Cute boys sometimes kiss not-cute girls. (This gives me hope!)

2. Cleo has some kind of charm that makes boys like her, though I have no idea WHAT.

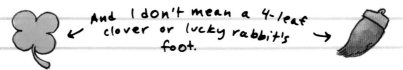

And I don't mean a 4-leaf ← clover or lucky rabbit's → foot.

3. Kids may like gossip about kids kissing, but grown-ups DO NOT! (I don't know if they like rumors about grown-ups kissing, but they sure don't like the ones about kids kissing.)

This isn't the kind of test that has right or wrong answers. It's the kind researchers use to learn about a subject, so don't worry about saying the wrong thing. Anyway, with gossip there is no right or wrong, just more or less believable.

I learned a _lot_ of lessons from gossip — not just about Cleo, but about Mr.L., and, most of all, about ME. I learned I'm the kind of person who HATES to be gossiped about. It's not fun or exciting, like I thought it might be. It's ICKY!

And the only way to stop a rumor once it's started is with the truth. I need to find out who really told on the e-mail girl.

The question is how am I supposed to do that?

Okay, I need a break from rumors, so it's time for a different kind of test. Again, there are no right answers, but there are <u>revealing</u> ones. Take this test to see

WHAT KIND OF GOSSIP ARE YOU?

3. When you have a particularly juicy piece of gossip, you...

ⓐ ... tell it only to your friends.

ⓑ ... rush off to repeat it to the first person you see.

ⓒ ... blurt it out at the wrong moment.

4. You know a lot of gossip about...

ⓐ ... who likes who.

ⓑ ... odd details about people.

ⓒ ... history.

5. Your reputation as a gossip is . . .

ⓐ . . . locked lips.

ⓑ . . . not the most exciting.

ⓒ . . . big blabber.

6. The longest you've been able to sit on a particularly juicy bit of news is . . .

ⓐ . . . one day.

ⓑ . . . one hour.

ⓒ . . . one second.

7. Your attitude toward the expiration date on gossip is...

(a) ... there's no point in not telling things right away — gossip goes stale so quickly.

(b) ... if it's just a little stale, it still can be served up.

(c) ... you mean there's an expiration date?

Now, this is fresh, fresh, fresh!

Dish, dish, dish!

This is a little chewy, but still worth sinking your teeth into.

I'm not so sure.

Listen! This happened a decade ago and it's HOT!

I can't hear you — tra la la!

8. The most important thing you learned from gossip is...

(a) ... popularity doesn't necessarily last long.

(b) ... nerds can be happy people too.

(c) ... no one wants to hear old news.

It's risky being the ultracool kids — better to be just below them in rank.

It's more stable.

A new calculator game is all it takes for complete happiness.

Wow — look how this works!

It's a shame because I have a juicy tidbit about the War of 1812 — it's HOT!

If you answered mostly a's, you're considered a person who understands the shifting, intricate relationships that make some gossip matter more than others. You're close enough to the cool kids to be cool yourself.

If you answered mostly b's, you're close to the middle of things on the gossip ripple effect chart, though not in the center. You like gossip, but you have a ways to go before you become an expert.

If you answered mostly c's, people don't tell you their secrets because they're not safe with you. You love gossip so much, you want to spread it all the time. Hey, this person is the **real** culprit in the mean e-mail girl rumor — not me! How do I figure out who answered mostly c's? Only a person who answered mostly a's can tell me!

← What does an "a" person look like? What does → a "c" look like?

I wish I could say I'm in the "a" category, but I'm more in the "b" group. I like gossip (when it's not about me), but I'm not very good at it. To be a grade A gossip, you need to know stuff _and_ you need to know how to tell it in an exciting way. The best gossip in school is Shawna. I wonder if _she_ knows the truth behind the rumor about me.

It's the way she tells you the item — like it's a big secret that only you get to hear, and even though you know she's probably told a million other people, you still feel special. Besides, she only tells quality gossip — the really interesting kind. She leaves the so-so stories to people like me.

You've got to hear the latest about Charisse. This is HOT off the gossip stove!

You know how Max has a crush on Charisse? Well, _she_ knows it too. She sent him an anonymous note telling him that a certain someone likes him the way he likes _her_.

Of course, that drove Max crazy! He was following Charisse all over the place, hoping to get a chance to talk to her alone. But Charisse just wanted to torment him — she made sure that never happened.

Then, when he was about to give up, she sent him a second note, saying the same thing, only with passion plus!

You can just imagine poor Max! That girl was leading him along by the nose!

Finally, Carly had pity on the poor boy and told him Charisse was just fooling with him. That was the end of that crush — now he hates her! Can you blame him?

Note how she describes a whole dramatic saga, the ups and downs, the pacing of it all — she's a master!

The BIGGEST gossip (not necessarily the best — they're two different things) is Maya. She ALWAYS has a story to share, some juicy, some not-so-juicy, some completely dried-up, but what she lacks in quality, she makes up for in quantity. This can be a good thing and a bad one. If you don't want it spread all over the school, watch what you say to Maya! (And if you want to spread a rumor fast, tell her first.) So maybe she knows who really told on the e-mail girl.

Are you ready for the rumor of the day?

Have you heard about Mr. Lambaste and the way he handcuffs kids? I swear, it's the truth!

Oh, you've heard that — stale news, I see. Well, I heard something else I'm sure you <u>don't</u> know about. You know the toilet in the bathroom that everyone avoids? The new French kid hadn't heard the rumor and ooh-la-la, quelle disastre! (That's French for "What a disaster!") You could <u>smell</u> the kid coming 3 hallways away because of the gross gunk on her shoes!

The worst gossip is Leah. Not because she's boring or tells really old, stale stories. Not because she can't tell juicy gossip from a dry shopping list (there are some people like that), but because she always forgets some crucial bit of information. It's <u>so</u> frustrating! Like if she knew who had really told on the girl for sending mean e-mails, she'd forget some major detail — like the kid's name!

There's no point in even asking her about the e-mail rumor.
Wait—was it Lucy this happened to—or Shelly?
Come to think of it, it was a boy. Yes, it was Omar!
So Omar said to Mr. Klein—no, it was Mr. Le Poivre. Anyway, he said to this teacher (whoever it was, I'm not sure), "I can't hand in my homework because my dog ate it." Of course, the teacher didn't believe him and was very angry. So he... um... the teacher... give me a second, I'll remember... Oh, wait, you wanted to know about those e-mails, right? That's something else!
Forget about it!
I'm getting a headache on top of my headache!

I'm better than Leah, but I'm a "pass it on" type of gossip. I hear something and I pass it on to my friends. I never get the scoop — the first news of something. And I don't always pass things on. I know when to keep my mouth shut and I'm good at keeping secrets.

At least I'm not a <u>mean</u> gossip — that's a completely different kind of thing. I'm just spreading valuable information. Okay, I admit I've said bad things about Mr. Lambaste — and about Cleo, too — but nothing that wasn't 100% certifiably true. (Okay, maybe the handcuffs weren't true in <u>fact</u>, but they were in <u>spirit</u>.) I don't spread nasty opinions, only objective facts. It's not my fault if Cleo gets carsick all the time. I don't tell her to chew with her mouth open or sing off-key in a screechy voice. But once she does, I <u>do</u> tell other people about it.

I <u>don't</u> tell personal secrets about her that no one else knows. And I could.

That's my list of private stuff that only someone who lives with Cleo could know about. If I write them down (and I just did), I have to black them out, and I would NEVER say them to anyone. Well, maybe only to Carly because she's my best friend. And I know she's not a gossip. But she told me something GREAT this morning— I'm not being gossiped about anymore! And I didn't even have to get the truth from Shawna or Maya. Instead, the truth came to <u>me</u>.

Here's the story (<u>true</u> gossip, not a false rumor): It was a <u>mom</u> who told the principal about the nasty e-mails. It wasn't even a kid. And yes, it was Shawna who found out the details first. Some parent was snooping on her kid's computer and found a really ugly message the girl had sent (she even signed her name!). She went right to the principal the next day.

I gave Carly a big hug. "My name's been cleared!" I said.

Carly smiled. "Yeah, you don't have to hide in the library at lunch anymore. But NOW will you admit gossip can be dangerous?"

I know, I know. It's like a bright flame — you can't take your eyes away, but you'd better not get too close.

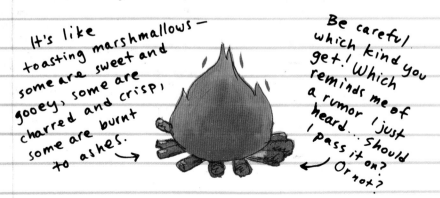

It's like toasting marshmallows — some are sweet and gooey, some are charred and crisp, some are burnt to ashes. →

Be careful which kind you get! Which reminds me of a rumor I just heard... Should I pass it on? Or not?